07/2021

The MAGNIFICENT MAKERS

How to Test a Friendship

Go on more
a-MAZE-ing adventures with

The
MAGNIFICENT
MAKERS

How to Test a Friendship
Brain Trouble
Riding Sound Waves

The MAGNIFICENT MAKERS 1

How to Test a Friendship

by Theanne Griffith
illustrated by Reggie Brown

A STEPPING STONE BOOK™
Random House New York

Text copyright © 2020 by Theanne Griffith
Cover art and interior illustrations copyright © 2020 by Reginald Brown

Visit us on the Web!
rhcbooks.com

Educators and librarians, for a variety of teaching tools, visit us at
RHTeachersLibrarians.com

Library of Congress Cataloging-in-Publication Data
Names: Griffith, Theanne, author. | Brown, Reggie, illustrator.
Title: How to test a friendship / by Theanne Griffith ;
illustrations by Reggie Brown.
Description: New York : Random House, [2020]
Series: The magnificent makers ; #1 | "A Stepping Stone book."
Summary: With the help of a fun, odd scientist, third graders Violet, Pablo, and
Deepak embark on an adventure in the Maker Maze, a magical laboratory
full of robots, an antigravity chamber, 3-D printers, and more.
Identifiers: LCCN 2019020356 (print) | LCCN 2019020582 (ebook) |
ISBN 978-0-593-12298-3 (trade pbk.) | ISBN 978-0-593-12299-0 (lib. bdg.) |
ISBN 978-0-593-12300-3 (ebook)
Subjects: CYAC: Science—Fiction. | Makerspaces—Fiction. |
Friendship—Fiction. | Schools—Fiction. | Magic—Fiction.
Classification: LCC PZ7.1.G7527 Ho 2020 (print) | LCC PZ7.1.G7527 (ebook)
DDC [Fic]—dc23

Printed in the United States of America
10 9 8 7 6 5 4 3 2

First Edition

This book has been officially leveled by using
the F&P Text Level Gradient™ Leveling System.

Random House Children's Books supports the
First Amendment and celebrates the right to read.

For Stephanie.
Thanks for being so nice
to this new kid.
—T.G.

For Demi. Thanks for letting me
watch anime when you're not home.
Love you more.
—R.B.

Pens and pencils? Check! Erasers? Check! Notebook? Check!

Pablo hopped in front of the mirror hanging on his bedroom door. The spaceship design on his new T-shirt matched the spaceships on his new sneakers. They were perfect for an astronaut-in-training. Awesome first-day-of-school outfit? Check!

Third grade, here I come! Pablo hurried downstairs. His parents were waiting for him by the front door.

"Are you ready?" asked his dad. He handed Pablo his spaceship lunch box.

"Yeah!" Pablo replied.

When Pablo and his parents arrived at Newburg Elementary, he saw his best friend. It was easy to spot Violet in a crowd. She was tall and had a head full of tightly coiled, dark brown curls.

Pablo and Violet had been best friends since he first moved to Newburg from Puerto Rico two years ago. They both loved the color red and playing soccer during recess. They both loved pickles but hated cucumbers. And they both *really* loved science. One day Pablo was going to fly a spaceship, just like the one on his shirt. Violet was going to discover cures for all kinds of diseases when she grew up.

"Hey, Violet! We got the same teacher again!" said Pablo.

"I know!" replied Violet. Her nose wiggled with excitement.

"You two have a great first day! And don't get into too much trouble." Pablo's mom winked.

"We won't!" Pablo and Violet replied.

They headed into their classroom. The desks were arranged in groups of three.

"Yes!" Violet cried. "We're sitting in the same group."

Pablo read the name tag on the third desk. "Deepak. Who is that?"

Violet shrugged.

DING, DING, DING! Their teacher rang the bell on his desk.

"Welcome, everyone. I'm Mr. Eng. I've planned a lot of fun activities this year."

There was a knock at the classroom door. It was the principal, Mrs. Jenkins. "Sorry to interrupt, Mr. Eng," she said. "There's one more student joining your class

4

today. He's new and got a little lost this morning. This is Deepak."

A boy with straight black hair stepped from behind Mrs. Jenkins.

"Look!" Violet whispered to Pablo.

Pablo turned in his chair. "What's the big deal?" he said. Then he saw it. *No way,* he thought.

Deepak was wearing the exact same shirt and shoes as Pablo. Pablo's first-day-of-school outfit didn't feel so special anymore.

"Hi, Deepak. My name is Violet. This is Pablo." Violet smiled as Deepak sat down. "Stick with us and we'll make sure you don't get lost again!"

Pablo wasn't smiling. "I'm Violet's best friend," he blurted out. His brown cheeks turned a little red.

"Cool! We have the same shirt, Pablo," said Deepak. "*And* shoes!"

"Yeah," muttered Pablo.

"Okay, class." Mr. Eng tapped a pencil on his desk. "It's time to get started."

Pablo turned away from Deepak to listen to their teacher.

"We're going to begin the year by learning about ecosystems," said Mr. Eng. "An ecosystem is an environment made up of living things, like plants and animals, and nonliving things, like rocks, water, and air." Mr. Eng pointed to the back of the room with his pencil. "Why don't we head over to the Science Space to learn more about them?"

"Yay!" Pablo and Violet said together.

"Is science your favorite subject?" Deepak asked Violet.

"Yup!" she replied. "I'm going to be the boss of a big laboratory one day!"

"I like science, too!" said Deepak.

"Vamos, Violet," Pablo interrupted. He grabbed his best friend's hand. "Let's go." They headed toward the back of the room.

Pablo and Violet couldn't wait to explore the Science Space. Along the wall was a shelf holding plastic bins filled with safety goggles, magnifying glasses, magnets, scales for weighing, and wooden boards with nuts and bolts for building. There were even two red drones!

"Oh, man! When are we going to get to fly those?" asked Pablo.

"I can't wait to learn how to program them! I bet they can do all kinds of cool tricks," said Violet.

They sat down at one of the tables in the Science Space. Deepak joined them. Mr. Eng passed around a handout.

Food Chain Fun

A **food chain** is how energy from food is passed from one living thing to another in an ecosystem.

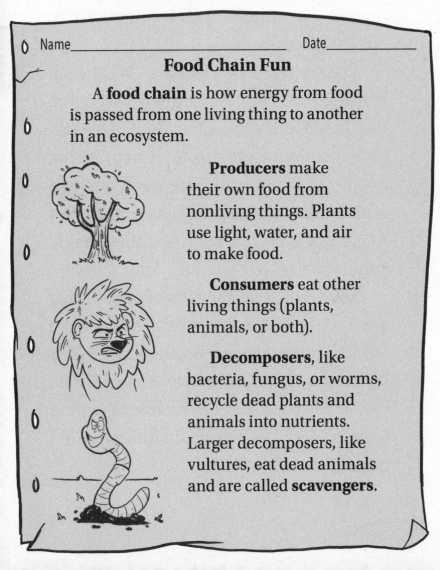

Producers make their own food from nonliving things. Plants use light, water, and air to make food.

Consumers eat other living things (plants, animals, or both).

Decomposers, like bacteria, fungus, or worms, recycle dead plants and animals into nutrients. Larger decomposers, like vultures, eat dead animals and are called **scavengers**.

"Think about the town of Newburg," said Mr. Eng. "You have ten minutes to make a list of living things that are producers, consumers, and decomposers in our local ecosystem."

Violet turned to Deepak. "We'll help you since you're new to town," she said. But Pablo didn't want to help Deepak. Then something got his attention. Sitting in the window of the Science Space was a shiny new telescope. Pablo had a small handheld telescope at home. But this one came with a fancy tripod!

Pablo decided to sneak over and take a peek. He was about to peep through the lens when a crumpled ball of paper rolled up next to him. He looked around. The rest of the class was busy working on the assignment. He picked up the crinkled paper ball and opened it.

M

PRODUCERS, CONSUMERS,
DECOMPOSERS, OH MY!
ALL ARE NECESSARY FOR AN
ECOSYSTEM TO SURVIVE.
MOST ANIMALS ARE _____.
LIVING THINGS, BEWARE!
IF _____ DISAPPEARED, WE
WOULDN'T HAVE FRESH AIR.
AND WITHOUT _____,
NATURE'S GARBAGE WOULD BE
EVERYWHERE!
SOLVE THIS RIDDLE TO ENTER THE
MAKER MAZE.

The Maker Maze? Pablo had gone through a corn maze at Newburg Farm. And a mirror maze at the Newburg Fair. But he had never heard of the Maker Maze.

"Hey, you guys! Look at this," said Pablo. He tossed the paper onto the table. Violet read it aloud.

She bit her lip. "Let's solve the riddle!"

"Wait," said Deepak. He pulled on his ear. He seemed a little unsure.

"What's the matter?" Pablo asked. "You aren't scared, *are you?*"

"No!" Deepak frowned.

"Come on, guys," said Violet. "I bet Mr. Eng is secretly passing these around. Maybe if we solve it first, we get a prize or something!"

The three kids stared at the wrinkly piece of paper.

"*Living things, beware,*" Violet read. She bit her lip again. "The first one must be consumers. They eat living things."

"Yeah," said Pablo. "And the handout says decomposers eat

dead stuff. So they're probably the ones who get rid of nature's garbage."

"We have lots of plants at home. My dad says they keep the air clean. I guess that means we have fresh air thanks to producers?" asked Deepak.

Before Pablo or Violet could answer, their chairs and table started to shake. Everything in the classroom was shaking! Then, as quickly as it had started, the shaking stopped.

"Whoa!" Pablo shouted. "Did you feel that?" Violet and Deepak nodded. Deepak gripped the table with trembling hands.

Every person in the classroom was frozen in place! They were as still as statues. Not even Mr. Eng budged!

BOOM! SNAP! WHIZ! ZAP!

"Look!" said Violet, pointing toward the window. The telescope was glowing inside a circle of purple light. They tip-toed toward it. Violet reached out and ran her fingers through the light. *BIZZAP!*

She giggled. "It tickles." They heard another noise behind them. They spun around. A pencil was rolling on the floor near Mr. Eng.

"It must have fallen from his ear. Every-one is still frozen," said Violet quietly.

"Can I see?" asked Pablo. He bent over and looked through the telescope. The purple light prickled his ears. *BIZZAP!*

Pablo didn't see the sky or any clouds. Instead, he saw some kind of laboratory. There were flasks lined up on a lab bench with different-color liquids bubbling inside them. Suddenly, something inside the telescope tugged at his shirt. He tried to pull away.

"Help!" Pablo cried.

He reached for his friends' hands. He was being sucked into the telescope! Violet dug her heels into the floor, but it was no use. It was as if they were paper clips, and the telescope was a giant magnet. One by one, Pablo, Deepak, and Violet were squeezed through. They fell for a few seconds, then landed in the lab with a thud.

The room was huge. Next to the flasks were rows of strange plants. One of the plants had leaves that moved all by themselves! Across from the strange plants were several giant jars holding creepy bugs. In one corner of the room, robots were organizing chemicals on a shelf.

"Whoa!" Violet exclaimed. "I could use robots like them when I have a lab!"

Deepak turned his head

to the side. "Is that plant dancing?"

There was also a row of clear boxes with various colorful crystals in them. And the crystals were floating!

"Those must be zero gravity chambers!" said Pablo.

"And over there!" Violet pointed to a microscope that was hooked up to a computer. "I bet I could see all kinds of bacteria and viruses with that."

Next to the microscope was a hallway lined with doors. It was so long it was impossible to tell where it ended.

"So I guess this is—" started Deepak.

"The Maker Maze!" called a voice from behind them.

They spun around. A tall woman with wild rainbow hair was standing in front

of them. She was wearing a white lab coat and bright purple pants. She held a large golden book under her arm. A pencil was tucked behind her ear.

"It's so wonderful to finally meet you!" said the woman as she clapped her hands. "You must be Pablo, Violet, and Deepak."

"How do you . . . ?" began Pablo.

"I always know the names of the people I invite to the Maze." She winked. "I'm Dr. Crisp." She pointed to the name tag on her lab coat. "Now let's get started! We have a lot to do before the others wake up."

"**S**o, what exactly *is* the Maker Maze?" asked Deepak.

"The Maker Maze is like a maker-space," replied Dr. Crisp. "But . . . with a little twist."

"You mean a *big* twist?" said Pablo. He was still in shock. Last year, their class had gone to a makerspace for a field trip. Pablo and Violet actually got to do experiments themselves! They built a bridge out of plastic cups and Popsicle sticks. And they tested which combination of vinegar and baking soda could make a bottle rocket fly the highest. Pablo was sure his rocket could have flown into space if it hadn't been for the ceiling.

But the Maker Maze was different. It was bigger and had *way* more fancy gadgets.

Dr. Crisp showed them the book she was holding. It was a bright, glittery shade of gold. Pablo reached out and touched it. **BIZZAP!** It prickled his fingers the way the purple light around the telescope had prickled his ears.

"Just tell the Maker Manual what you want to learn about," Dr. Crisp said. "The Maze will design a challenge, and you'll have one hundred twenty Maker Minutes to complete it."

"One hundred twenty Maker Minutes?" repeated Violet.

"You bet your pipette!" answered Dr. Crisp. "That's how long the Maze will keep your classmates frozen." She pointed with her pencil to a screen above them. They could see their classroom, where everyone was as still as stone.

"And when time runs out?" asked Deepak. He gulped.

Dr. Crisp sighed. "If you can't finish in time, I won't be able to invite you back. Maker Maze rules," she said, tapping the manual.

"Is it really hard?" asked Pablo.

"Don't fret, space cadet! I choose my Makers wisely. I know you all are up for the challenge!" said Dr. Crisp. She opened the golden book to a page with just one giant question mark on it. "Who'd like to suggest a topic?" she asked, smiling.

"Wait. We're not going to have to do anything dangerous, are we?" asked Pablo.

"Oh, Pablo, don't be a party pooper! What's the worst that could happen?" said Violet. Deepak giggled.

"You'll be safer here than in outer space!" said Dr. Crisp. She made an *M* with her three middle fingers facing down. "Maker's honor," she promised.

Pablo stared at the spaceships on his sneakers. "Okay," he said. "Let's learn about ecosystems."

Nothing happened. The trio looked at Dr. Crisp. She was still smiling. Suddenly, the pages of the Maker Manual began to turn. They turned slowly at first. One by one. Then faster. And faster! It looked like a tornado was spinning through the book. Finally, they stopped. The page read:

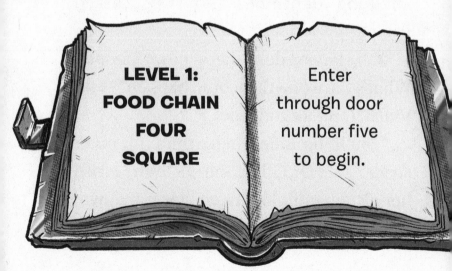

LEVEL 1: FOOD CHAIN FOUR SQUARE

Enter through door number five to begin.

Dr. Crisp snapped the book shut, grabbed a backpack, and put the Maker Manual inside. "Follow me!" she said, and took off sprinting down the long hallway.

"Wait up!" shouted Violet.

They ran as fast as they could. They passed doors number one, two, three, and four. Dr. Crisp was waiting for them at door number five.

"Here we go!" said Dr. Crisp. She reached for the doorknob.

"Hold on!" said Pablo. "How will we keep track of Maker Minutes?"

"With your Magnificent Maker Watches, of course!" said Dr. Crisp.

"Our what?" asked Violet.

Dr. Crisp pointed to the black watches on their wrists.

"Wow, these are cool!" said Violet.

The watches had touch screens and a few small buttons. Dr. Crisp was wearing one, too.

"How did these get on our wrists?" Pablo whispered.

But Dr. Crisp didn't hear him. "Let's go, Makers!" she said. Their watches vibrated and glowed as they walked through door number five. The challenge had begun.

"**O**uch!" One of Violet's curls was tangled in a tree branch. Pablo went over to help her.

"This doesn't look like a maze. We're in the Newburg Forest," said Violet. "How did we get here?" Door number five was gone. They were standing in the middle of a trail.

Dr. Crisp tapped the screen on her watch three times and swiped left. The forest slid away. They were in a huge white room, and door number five was behind them. "The Maze can make a clone of any place in the world!" Dr. Crisp explained. "But it's only a copy." She tapped her watch three times and swiped right. The forest glided back into view.

"Wow!" the trio said all at once. This *was* a special makerspace.

"I never thought I would have such a fun first day of school!" said Deepak.

"Yeah, me neither," agreed Pablo. He smiled and patted Deepak on the back.

The group followed the trail until it ended at an open field.

"Here we are!" said Dr. Crisp.

"*This* is it?" asked Violet. She squinted and pushed a few lose kinks of hair out of her face. She saw nothing but trees, grass, and a few scattered dandelions.

BOOM! SNAP! WHIZ! ZAP!

Pablo, Violet, and Deepak squeezed their eyes shut. A flash of purple light blinded them. When the light faded, there was a giant game board on the ground that looked like a tablet screen. It was divided into four squares. Pablo pointed his foot toward one of them. It lit up with a tap of his toe.

Dr. Crisp explained the rules. "Listen up, Makers! A hologram of a living thing from the Newburg Forest ecosystem will appear in the center of the board." Dr. Crisp pointed at the trio with her pencil. "It's up to you to decide what role it plays in the forest food chain. Then you have to move the hologram to the correct square." Floating words and symbols hovered over each section of the board:

consumer

producer

decomposer

scavenger

"One more thing," Dr. Crisp added. "You won't be able to move the hologram unless you *all* agree on which square it belongs in. Whenever you're ready, Makers!"

The word *go* appeared on their watches. They all tapped them at the same time.

A hologram of a fox hovered over the middle of the board.

"This one is easy!" said Violet. "Foxes are predators. They hunt other animals. It must be a consumer." Deepak and Pablo nodded.

Violet reached for the fox.

"Be careful!" Deepak shouted.

Pablo laughed. "¿Qué pasa? It's a hologram, *remember?*"

Deepak blushed with embarrassment.

Violet pulled Pablo close and whispered, "Why are you being so mean?"

"I'm not," Pablo replied. He shook her off. As he walked toward the fox, it growled.

"Whoa!" Pablo cried.

Violet and Deepak laughed quietly.

"Don't worry, Pablo!" said Dr. Crisp "It can't hurt you!" She signed the Maker's honor.

Pablo took a deep breath and grabbed the fox. *BIZZAP!* He put it in the consumer square. The square flashed purple.

RING, DING, DONG!

"One down, three to go!" shouted Dr. Crisp. "Hurry, hurry, Makers! Don't be too slow!"

A group of mushrooms appeared.

"Those must be producers!" said Pablo.

"I don't know," said Violet. She explained that mushrooms grew in the compost pile in her backyard. "My dad says the mushrooms help break down the compost."

"I think they're decomposers," suggested Deepak.

Violet agreed.

"But mushrooms are plants. And plants are *producers*." Pablo tapped his foot impatiently.

"Actually, mushrooms are a kind of fungus," said Deepak quietly. "I learned about them at science camp over the summer."

But Pablo wouldn't give in.

"Come on, Pablo. It's two against one. We can't move them unless you agree with us," Violet said.

Pablo shrugged.

Violet tried to grab the hologram. Her hands passed right through the bunch of mushrooms.

Pablo checked his watch. One hundred Maker Minutes left.

100 min. left

M

"Fine," he mumbled. "Mushrooms are decomposers."

Violet reached for the mushrooms. This time she could pick them up.

RING, DING, DONG!

A fern plant appeared on the game board. That was easy. "Producer!" the trio yelled out. Deepak set the fern in the producer square.

Then a hologram of a crow popped up. There was only one square left.

"Crows are scavengers?" Pablo asked aloud.

"I once saw a bunch of crows eating roadkill," added Violet. "It was pretty gross."

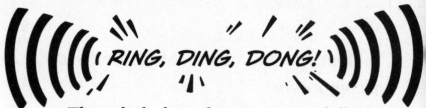

RING, DING, DONG!

The whole board game started flash-ing purple.

"Bada, bam, boom!" said Dr. Crisp as she played an imaginary drum set. "You've mastered the first level, Makers!" She hopped up on the board and gave everyone high fives with her invisible drumstick.

Violet and Deepak hugged. Pablo was happy they beat the level, too. But for some reason, he didn't really feel like celebrating.

"Okay, Makers, let's see where the Maze sends us next!" said Dr. Crisp.

She grabbed the Maker Manual out of her backpack. It flew open, and the pages began turning. When they stopped, the page read:

LEVEL 2: ON THE HUNT

Go to Newburg Lake.

"Forward, march!" Dr. Crisp began stomping toward the lake.

Violet grabbed Deepak's hand and dashed after Dr. Crisp. Pablo watched his best friend and Deepak run off. He dragged his feet as he followed them.

When they got to the lake, Dr. Crisp

asked, "Who's ready to go on a scavenger hunt?" She winked. "But not just for scavengers!"

The kids smiled and raised their hands. Dr. Crisp pressed a button on her watch and projected a list into the air for everyone to see.

"You have to find each of these in order to complete the level. You'll also have to decide where they fit in the ecosystem," said Dr. Crisp. "But first," she added, holding her finger in the air, "you will need to make a boat."

1. Crayfish
2. Water lily
3. Frog

"Oh, cool!" said Violet.

"But we're just kids. How can we make a boat?" asked Deepak.

"You aren't just kids," replied Dr. Crisp. "You're Makers!"

She opened the Maker Manual to a picture of a plastic-bottle boat with a list of instructions. As Pablo, Violet, and Deepak read them, Dr. Crisp reached into her backpack. "Stand back!" She tossed her rainbow hair out of the way and started grunting and making strange noises. Then she slowly pulled a giant plastic bottle out of her bag. It was the size of a small school bus! The trio's mouths fell open.

"You had that in there the whole time? But how?" asked Pablo.

Dr. Crisp just kept digging. She pulled out some glue, three large rubber bands, two long pieces of wood, and two big plastic spoons.

"I need a backpack like that!" said Violet.

Dr. Crisp turned toward the Makers with a big smile. She raised both hands over her head and then lowered them quickly. "Ready, set, MAKE!"

Pablo, Violet, and Deepak got to work. First, they had to attach the two pieces of wood to the plastic bottle using rubber bands.

Violet bit her lip. "I have an idea. Give me a hand!" she said to Pablo and Deepak.

They laid the two pieces of wood on the ground and rolled the giant bottle on top. Some of the wood stuck out behind the bottle.

"That's where the motor has to go," said Violet, looking at the instructions.

Pablo picked up one of the bands. "Are these going to be big enough?" he asked. The rubber bands were big, but not *that* big.

Dr. Crisp slid into a yoga position. "Looks like you'll have to give them a *stretch*!" she said, arching her back in cobra pose.

Pablo pulled the band a few times to loosen it up. "Somebody will need to climb on top to help get the rubber band over the bottle," he said.

"I'll do it!" said Deepak.

"Are you sure? You might fall. *SPLAT!*" said Pablo, clapping his hands together loudly.

"Pablo!" Violet frowned.

Deepak focused on the bottle. Then he ran and jumped as high as he could. He

landed smack on the side and started to slip.

"Be careful!" shouted Violet.

Deepak gripped the bottle tightly. He slithered up the side and made his way to the top.

"Jumping bell jars!" cheered Dr. Crisp.

"You did it, Deepak!" said Violet.

Pablo kicked at some rocks on the ground. "It wasn't even that high," he mumbled.

Violet turned to Pablo. "Then why didn't *you* go up there? How will you make it to space if you won't even jump off the ground?"

"I'll use my spaceship!" Pablo yelled back. But Violet was already heading toward the bottle.

"Come on!" she said over her shoulder.

Pablo and Violet were able to get the

rubber band around the free ends of wood without any trouble.

Violet squatted down and gripped the rubber band. "Now get on my shoulders," she said to Pablo.

"Huh?" he replied.

"Hurry!" she said.

Pablo climbed onto Violet. "Hey!" she screamed. "Watch out for my hair!"

"Sorry, *jeez,*" he said.

Violet pulled the rubber band up over her head and passed it to Pablo.

"You have to stretch it enough so Deepak can grab it," she told him.

Deepak lay over the edge of the bottle and reached toward Pablo. Pablo stretched the band as much as he could.

"This thing is going to snap!" he grunted.

"Keep trying!" said Violet.

Pablo pulled even harder. Somehow he managed to get the rubber band into Deepak's hands. Thank goodness Violet was so tall! Pablo hopped off her shoulders. They helped roll the rubber band around the bottle.

"Way to *band* together, Makers!" said Dr. Crisp.

The trio did the same for the second rubber band.

"Now we have to make the motor," said Pablo. He grabbed the big two spoons.

"Come on down, Deepak!" yelled Violet.

Violet and Deepak broke off the curved spoon heads. They glued them together with one facing up and the other facing down. Pablo tied the last rubber band tightly around the loose edges of the wood. Then they glued the spoon-head motor to the middle of the band.

(((((((RING, DING, DONG!)))))))

"Now, that's how you build a boat!" said Dr. Crisp. "All aboard, Makers!"

The trio ran to the bottle. Deepak climbed up easily. He turned around and pulled Violet up next to him. He tried to help Pablo up, too.

"I can do it by myself!" said Pablo as he made his way on top of the boat.

Dr. Crisp took a seat on the wood near the motor and wound it up. The boat shot out onto the water.

"Time to go overboard!" said Dr. Crisp. They had reached the middle of the lake.

"But, Dr. Crisp," said Violet, "we don't have bathing suits!"

"I'll take care of that!" Dr. Crisp laughed. Then she said into her watch, "Maker Maze, activate swim gear!"

Nothing happened.

"Oh, fiddle flasks," said Dr. Crisp. "I need a new watch."

She repeated the command.

BOOM! SNAP! WHIZ! ZAP!

Suddenly, Pablo, Violet, and Deepak were spinning. They spun faster and faster until they could barely see the lake!

"Whoaaaa! What's happening?" Pablo shouted.

Then they came to a sudden stop.

"I think I'm going to be sick," said Deepak, grabbing his stomach.

Violet giggled. "Let's do it again!"

"Look!" said Pablo, pointing at Violet and Deepak. They were all wearing wet suits. With flippers. *And* scuba gear!

"Okay, hop to it!" said Dr. Crisp. She showed the trio two small buttons on the side of their Magnificent Maker Watches. One was for scanning, and the other was for talking to one another underwater.

Then she gave them one last tip.

"Remember, living things live close to what they eat. That's why it's called a food chain. Everything in an ecosystem is linked together by food." She winked. "Good luck, Makers!"

Violet wobbled to the edge of the boat.

Pablo laughed. "You're walking like a penguin!"

"Let's see you try it!" Violet called back as she hopped overboard. Deepak followed her.

Pablo dove in. He swam to the bottom of the lake. It was covered with mud, twigs, and rocks. Then he saw something out of the corner of his eye. It looked like a little lobster. But there weren't any lobsters in Newburg Lake. He swam closer. It was a crayfish!

SNAP!

Yikes! Pablo thought. The crayfish tried to pinch him! He backed off. Pablo waved to Violet and Deepak as he pointed at the feisty creature. They smiled through their scuba gear. Pablo aimed his watch at the crayfish. Out blasted a purple laser! It scanned the crayfish, and his watch vibrated. A large check mark appeared on the screen. Pablo's stomach felt bubbly with excitement. The trio celebrated with high fives.

A flashing arrow blinked on Pablo's watch. He swiped it. The word *producer* appeared. He swiped again. *Consumer.* And finally, *scavenger.*

"Which one is it?" asked Violet into her watch.

Pablo knew the answer. Back in Puerto Rico, the stream that ran behind his house was full of crayfish. He loved watching the crayfish scuttle

around. His mom called them the basureros del arroyo, the stream's garbage collectors. They ate rotting leaves and twigs. They also ate dead fish. One time he saw a crayfish eating a minnow's head!

"Crayfish are scavengers!" Pablo said. "That's why you find them in the mud. I bet they eat all the dead stuff that falls to the bottom of the lake."

Deepak shook his head. "We had a pet crayfish in my class last year," he said. "The teacher would feed it tiny fish. And the crayfish would hunt them. That means crayfish are *consumers*."

"Nope," said Pablo. "Crayfish are *scavengers*."

"Guys, we're scientists. We can figure this out," said Violet.

Pablo's nostrils flared. "I know the answer!"

"We should make sure we're right," said Violet. "Deepak has a point."

Pablo's excitement was turning into bubbles of anger. He faced Deepak. "You think you know everything! But you don't. You don't know anything. The only thing you know is how to steal best friends!" Pablo shouted. He swam off.

Violet called out to him to wait. But Pablo was already far away.

Pablo swam and swam. Violet and Deepak could figure out the rest of the challenge all by themselves. He was going to find Dr. Crisp and demand to go back. He wanted out of the Maker Maze.

Pablo glanced over his shoulder but didn't see anyone. He was still looking back when he felt something slide along his arm. Then he saw something slide across the front of his helmet. He kicked his flippers harder. But after a few kicks, he could barely move his legs anymore.

He was tangled! *What is this stuff?* Pablo thought. They looked like skinny ropes. Maybe vines? Then Pablo realized what was wound so tightly around his arms and legs. He was trapped in long, twisted water lily roots.

"Help!" he screamed. His voice echoed

inside of his scuba gear. Violet and Deepak were too far away, and his arm was too tangled to use his watch.

Pablo started to panic. How was he going to escape? Would Dr. Crisp know something was wrong and come looking for him? The roots grew tighter around his arms and legs. Pablo needed Violet. But his best friend was nowhere to be found. *I should have stayed with the group,* he thought. Pablo closed his eyes and began to cry.

Pablo struggled to free himself from the roots. Suddenly, there was a tug at his ankle. Pablo tried to kick away whatever was pulling at him.

"Get off!" he shouted. He looked toward his flipper. But instead of some lake creature, he saw Violet and Deepak.

"Violet! You found me!" Pablo exclaimed. He had never been happier to see his best friend. She and Deepak worked together to untangle the roots.

"Stand up, Pablo!" Violet said into her watch.

Pablo didn't understand. *Stand up?* He looked down. He was only a couple of feet above the bottom of the lake. Pablo felt so embarrassed. He was in shallow water! Pablo stood up. Violet and Deepak did the same.

"I'm sorry, you guys. I shouldn't have left like that. I just got . . . well . . . I got jealous," he said. He turned to Deepak. "Violet has been my best friend since I came to Newburg. Back then *I* was the new kid. Now you're the new kid. You're smart. And you like science." Pablo paused, then said, "I was scared you were going to become her new best friend."

"Pablo, no one could ever replace you!" said Violet. She gave him a hug.

"I don't want to take your place, Pablo. I just want you guys to like me," said Deepak.

Pablo understood how that felt. He remembered trying really hard to make friends. "I'm sorry I wasn't more welcoming to you, Deepak."

"It's okay, Pablo. I'm glad we talked about this," Deepak said.

"Me too," agreed Violet. The three friends hugged one another tightly.

Pablo checked his watch. "We only have forty Maker Minutes left!"

Violet bit her lip. "Okay. Back to the challenge. We found water lilies. But we haven't finished crayfish yet. What if crayfish are scav-

engers *and* consumers?" she said. "Maybe their role in the food chain depends on where they live."

"That's a good idea!" said Pablo. He swiped his watch until the screen read *consumer*. He selected it. Nothing happened. He swiped again until he saw *scavenger*. Then he tapped the screen.

RING, DING, DONG!

"Whew! That was super hard," said Deepak. He wiped his forehead. "I'm glad we worked together to figure it out." He gave Pablo a pat on the back.

Violet activated her watch to scan a water lily. The group agreed it was a producer.

RING, DING, DONG!

They started to search for a frog.

"Over here!" Deepak shouted.

A little green frog was sitting in the center of a water lily. Just as Deepak was about to scan it, the frog hopped away.

"Oh no!" said Violet. They followed it carefully.

The frog settled on another water lily

with a pink flower blooming from its center. As Deepak aimed his watch, the frog opened its mouth. Out shot a long pink tongue. *Smack!* It landed right on a fly that was buzzing through the air.

"Its tongue moved so fast! That fly didn't stand a chance," said Pablo.

"No wonder frogs hang out here," Violet added. "The flowers attract bugs!"

Frogs were definitely consumers.

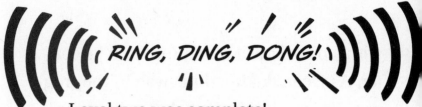

Level two was complete!

"Ahoy, Makers!" called a voice in the distance.

Dr. Crisp was heading toward them on the boat. She hopped off into the water. Her lab coat and bright purple pants got soaked, but she didn't seem to mind.

"Dr. Crisp, did you know that crayfish can be either scavengers *or* consumers?" asked Pablo. He was still amazed at their discovery.

"Living things are always adapting," explained Dr. Crisp. "Fish are very fast and hard to catch."

"So it's easier for crayfish to be scavengers in the wild?" asked Pablo.

"Precisely." Dr. Crisp winked. "In a

tank, crayfish will hunt. There is nowhere for fish to escape," she explained.

"That makes sense," replied Deepak.

Dr. Crisp paused as she took the Maker Manual out of her backpack. "You know, friend groups are a lot like ecosystems. Over time they can change. And that isn't always bad. Just like the crayfish, we have to learn to adapt."

"I learned that lesson the hard way," Pablo said, laughing. He reached out and put his arms around Violet and Deepak.

Dr. Crisp smiled as she held out the Maker Manual. It flipped open.

LEVEL 3: WHAT'S MISSING?

Go to Newburg Orchard.

"Follow me!" Dr. Crisp said. The trio started to wobble in their flippers.

"Dr. Crisp!" said Violet. She pointed to their wet suits. "Our clothes?"

"Oops!" Dr. Crisp laughed. "Maker Maze, deactivate swimwear!" she said into her watch.

"Not again," moaned Deepak as he closed his eyes.

"Wheeeeeee!" cried Violet. The trio started to spin. When they stopped, the wet suits, flippers, and scuba gear had disappeared.

"We only have thirty Maker Minutes!" Pablo said. "We better hurry."

30 min. left

M

"**W**elcome to Newburg Orchard," Dr. Crisp said. Pablo and Violet had been here many times with their families. They saw the familiar big red barn and silo. But the rest of the place didn't look anything like they remembered. In fact, it didn't look like much of an orchard at all.

"Is something wrong?" Deepak asked.

Pablo scratched his cheek. "It's normally full of colorful fruit trees." But these fields were dusty brown and covered in wheat.

Violet turned to Dr. Crisp. "Last year some of the trees in Newburg Forest got infected with nasty bacteria. My dad called it a yellow disease. I wanted to try to cure them." Violet crossed her arms and frowned. "But he didn't let me. Did the trees get some kind of disease?"

"Not this time," said Dr. Crisp. She took her pencil and pointed toward the wheat fields. "An important member of the Newburg Orchard ecosystem has vanished. And I'm not talking about the trees. It's up to you, Makers, to figure out who's missing."

Pablo, Violet, and Deepak set off to explore.

"Well," began Pablo, "fruit trees are plants."

"Maybe whatever is missing helps plants live," said Deepak.

"But not *all* plants are gone," observed Violet. The orchard was full of wheat.

"Look over there!" Pablo pointed behind the barn. There was a small plot of land with a few trees that were full of flowers. The trio ran over to investigate.

As they got closer, they could see people up in the trees. Each person was holding a paintbrush.

"What are they doing? Are they painting the flowers?" asked Pablo.

"That's weird," said Violet.

There was also a fruit stand near one of the trees with some pears on it.

"These must be pear trees," said Pablo. He turned to the people working in the trees. "Excuse me," he said. No one responded.

"Maybe they can't hear you," said Violet. She moved closer to the tree. "Excuse me!" she shouted.

Silence. Pablo saw a man coming down from one of the trees on a ladder. He walked over to him.

"Excuse me, can you . . . ?" Pablo tried to tap the man on his arm. *BIZZAP!* His finger went straight through him!

"Violet, Deepak, check this out!" Pablo shouted. He waved his hand through the man again. *BIZZAP!* "They're just holograms."

BIZZAP!

"That's kind of creepy," said Deepak.

Violet laughed. "Wow! Maybe that's why they can't talk." She took a few steps back, then started to run.

"Out of my way!" she said. She ran past Pablo and Deepak and straight through the hologram.

BIZZAP!

The man shivered and looked around. Deepak gasped.

"Look what you did," whispered Pablo. But the man continued on his way.

"Don't worry! It's just a little Maker Maze magic!" replied Violet. She shook her hands and giggled. "I'm all tingly!"

Pablo moved closer to one of the trees. A woman was dipping her paintbrush into the center of the flowers. The brush had some kind of yellow dust on it. What were they doing?

"**B**ees," Pablo said suddenly.

"What?" said Violet.

"Bees! I think that's who's missing," Pablo repeated. "The last time I came here, I got stung!" Pablo exclaimed. "By a bee!"

"So?" said Violet. "What do bees have to do with trees?"

"Bees spread pollen from flower to flower," said Pablo, pointing to a pear tree. "I think that's what those people are doing with the paintbrushes. Spreading the pollen since there are no bees to do it for them."

Violet crossed her arms. "I don't get it. What does spreading pollen have to do with whether the orchard has trees?"

Pablo looked at the ground. He wasn't sure.

Deepak tugged on his ear. "When pollen mixes between flowers, it makes seeds. It's called pollination," he said. "So maybe without the bees, the trees couldn't make more seeds!"

"And since fruit have seeds inside them, the trees must have stopped making fruit!" said Pablo. The two boys gave each other a double high five.

"That must be why there aren't so many trees anymore," added Deepak. "They stopped growing fruit, so the farmer stopped planting them!"

RING, DING, DONG!

"Yes!" they all shouted.

Pablo pointed to their watches. "Oh no!" he said. They only had ten Maker Minutes left. They hurried back to the entrance of the orchard.

Dr. Crisp was waiting for them.

"We figured it out!" exclaimed Violet. "Well, Pablo and Deepak figured it out. It was the bees! They were missing from the orchard."

"Bee-utiful job, Makers!" she said.

Pablo turned to Dr. Crisp. "You were right, Dr. Crisp. Being in a group of friends is like being part of an ecosystem. Each person is important." He looked at Deepak. "We made a really great team on this level! We couldn't have finished without you."

Deepak smiled.

"Why is the orchard covered with wheat?" asked Violet.

"Bees are important for pollinating trees that have fruit," explained Dr. Crisp. "But some plants use the wind instead of bees to spread pollen. Like wheat! Since there were no bees, the farmer planted wheat instead."

Dr. Crisp's watch started flashing with purple light. "Only three Maker Minutes left!" She tapped her watch three times and swiped left. The large white room slid into view.

In front of them was door number five. They darted through the door and ran down the hallway. Finally, they were back

in the main room. Creepy bugs still hissed in jars, and the crystals were still floating. Pablo, Violet, and Deepak looked up at the screen. Their classmates were still frozen. *Phew!*

"Thirty seconds!" yelled Dr. Crisp. "Jump!"

"Huh?" the trio said.

"JUMP! HURRY!" Dr. Crisp shouted, pointing to the circle of purple light glowing on the ceiling.

Pablo, Violet, and Deepak jumped. But they landed right back on the floor of the Maker Maze.

"HIGHER! YOU HAVE TO JUMP HIGHER!" screamed Dr. Crisp.

They jumped again with all their might.

BOOM! SNAP! WHIZ! ZAP!

The strong pull that had sucked them through the telescope now sucked them through the ceiling. They rolled onto the floor and crashed into their table and chairs just as everyone in the class unfroze.

"Hey, what are you doing down there?" Mr. Eng asked.

"Ummmm," said Pablo.

"Back in your seats, please," said Mr. Eng.

"Yes, Mr. Eng." Pablo, Violet, and Deepak picked themselves up and sat at their table.

Pablo looked around. "Did all that really happen?" he whispered.

Violet picked a piece of wheat out of Deepak's hair. "I think it did," she said with a smile.

Mr. Eng walked over to their group. Pablo squinted. Did Mr. Eng have a piece of wheat in his hair, too?

Mr. Eng squatted down and tapped his pencil on the table. "I'm sure you are having fun," he said, "but I hope you also did some good brainstorming."

"Oh, don't worry, Mr. Eng," said Violet. She winked at her friends. "We've got some a-MAZE-ing ideas." They all laughed.

Mr. Eng raised his eyebrows. "Good," he said as he stood up. "Science is fun, but it's also serious." He turned around and headed to another table.

"Mr. Eng is right," said Pablo, smiling. "Science is seriously fun!"

⪢MAKE A RUBBER BAND– POWERED BOAT!⪡

Always *make* carefully and with adult supervision!

MATERIALS

1 recycled 24-oz. plastic bottle with labels removed

2 pieces of wood (about 12 inches long and 1 inch wide)*

2 plastic spoons

3 rubber bands

scissors

superglue

*You can get creative and use rulers or even sticks! They just need to be fairly straight so you can glue them easily to the bottle.

INSTRUCTIONS

1. Apply superglue along one side of the bottle. Firmly press one piece of wood into the glue. About 4 to 6 inches of it should be hanging off the end.

2. Repeat on the opposite side and allow the glue to dry.

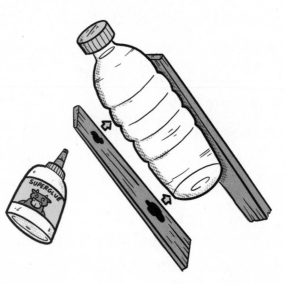

3. Wrap two rubber bands tightly around the bottle and wood. Set aside.

4. Use scissors to cut the spoon heads off, leaving about half of the handle attached.

5. Glue the spoon handles together, with one spoon head facing up and the other facing down.

6. Allow the glue to dry. This is your motor!

SNIP

YOUR MOTOR

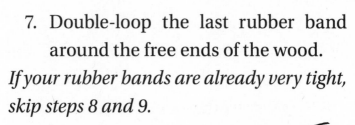

7. Double-loop the last rubber band around the free ends of the wood.

If your rubber bands are already very tight, skip steps 8 and 9.

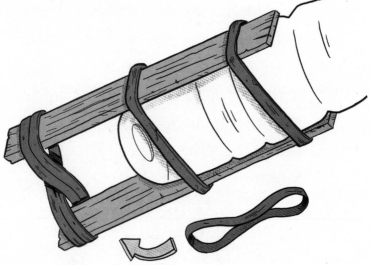

8. Grab the bottom-left side of the rubber band. Loop it one more time around the wood.

9. Flip the bottle over and repeat on the other side.

10. Place the motor in the gap between the top and bottom of the rubber band. Make sure the spoon head closest to the bottle is facing down. Wind the motor once. You may need to re-straighten the rubber band.

11. Glue both sides of the motor and rubber band together and allow to dry.

12. Find a water source (stream, pond, or even your bathtub). Wind up your motor and launch the boat!

13. When you've finished, remember to recycle!

Your parent or guardian can share pictures and videos of your boat on social media using #MagnificentMakers.

≥MAKE AN ECOSYSTEM OF YOUR OWN!≤

Create a diorama of any ecosystem you like! You can model a forest, rain forest, desert, etc. You can even make up your own ecosystem with fictional plants and animals! To make your diorama, use an empty shoe box or any other small (or big!)

box. Try to include three or more different types of animals and at least two different kinds of plants. Make sure to add some nonliving things, like rocks and soil. Get creative! You can use household materials or purchase supplies to make your diorama. Your parent or guardian can share your dioramas on social media using #MagnificentMakers.

Missing the
Maker Maze already?

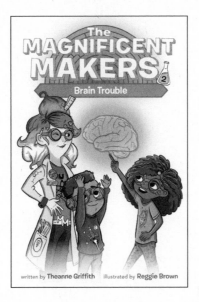

Read on for a peek at the
Magnificent Makers' next adventure!

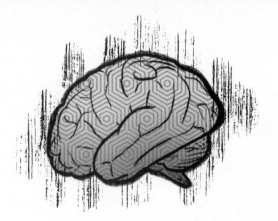

"**D**o you think there are *real* brains in there?" Violet whispered to her best friend, Pablo.

Pablo shivered. "Gross! Did you turn into a zombie or something?"

"Maybe I did. . . ." Violet raised her hands overhead and pretended to take a bite out of Pablo's shoulder. They laughed as they waited in line with the rest of their class.

It was brain awareness week at Newburg Elementary, and local college

students had organized a brain fair. No one knew exactly what it was—but they heard there would be tons of games and activities.

"I wonder if traveling to space messes with your brain," said Pablo, scratching his cheek. "Since there's no gravity and all."

"Maybe when you're an astronaut, I'll do some experiments and find out!" Violet replied, tapping the tips of her fingers together.

"No way!" Pablo laughed, covering his head with his hands.

Pablo and Violet had been best friends since first grade. They played on the same soccer team after school. And they both loved to order pickle pizza at the New-burg Diner. But what really made them best friends was how much they both loved science. Pablo was going to become an astronaut. Violet was going to run a lab of her own and study different kinds of diseases.

"Okay, students," said Mr. Eng from the front of the line. "It's almost time to go inside."

"Yay!" everyone cheered loudly.

Mr. Eng removed a pencil from his ear and put it in front of his lips. *"Shhhhhh!* We are still in the hallway and need to use our indoor voices."

The class settled down. But there was a buzz of excitement in the air.

Violet was the tallest and tried to peek through the window of the gym door. "All I see are a bunch of fourth and fifth

graders who look like they're having fun."
She crossed her arms and sighed. "When's
it going to be our turn?"

The gym doors opened, and out walked
Principal Jenkins.

"Good morning, students!" she said.

"Good morning, Principal Jenkins!" replied the class.

"I hope everyone is ready to learn all about the brain!" She waved the class into the gym with a warm smile.

"Come on, Pablo!" Violet grabbed his hand.

The gym was packed with different stations. At one, kids were making jiggly brain molds out of Jell-O. On the other side of the gym, a fifth grader was making a toy car move using cables attached to his arms. There was also a group of kids watching a cockroach leg dance to the beat of music playing on a cell phone. And at another station, a student wore a cap with a bunch of wires sticking out of it. It looked like they were recording signals from his brain!

"Violet, ¡mira!" said Pablo. He tugged on her shirt. "Look over there!"

Violet's eyes darted to where Pablo was pointing. On the opposite side of the room was a station with five red and silver microscopes lined up on a table. A smile grew on Violet's face. It stretched so wide it nearly touched each ear. Her fingers

started to jitter, and her eyes sparkled with amazement.

"Oooooooh!" Violet squealed. "I wonder if they're looking at brains!" She dashed toward the last open microscope.

But before she reached the station, a fourth grader swooped in and sat down.

"Hey!" Violet frowned. "I was going to sit there!"

"I got here first!" replied the fourth grader.

Violet wanted to cry. "This is so unfair," she said.

Just then Mr. Eng walked up behind Violet and Pablo. "Everything okay here?" he asked.

"I'm never going to be able to cure diseases if I don't get to practice using a microscope," said Violet, hanging her head.

"Don't worry. I'm sure you'll stumble across something even more exciting before the brain fair is over." Mr. Eng winked.

Pablo leaned in close to Violet and said, "Maybe *you know who* will send us another riddle today."

Violet lifted her head. The sparkle returned to her eyes.

Acknowledgments

Thank you, Jorge, for your unwavering encouragement. Dad, I am forever grateful that you instilled in me a love for books. All those trips to the public library really paid off! Thank you, Mom, for being my guardian angel. I wish you were here on earth with me to enjoy this journey. I never would have embarked on this adventure had you not taught me to chase my dreams fearlessly. Violeta and Lila, I love you both so much. You're a constant source of inspiration. Thank you to my critique group partners Annie, Christine, and Louise. You all are the best! Finally, thank you to my wonderful agent, Liza Fleissig; my amazing editor, Caroline Abbey; and the Random House team for your continued guidance and support.